Consider Love

To:

From:

DEDICATED
To
James Patrick George Jawbone McEwan

LITTLE SIMON
An imprint of Simon & Schuster Children's Publishing Division
1230 Avenue of the Americas, New York, New York 10020
Copyright © 2002 by Sandra Boynton
All rights reserved, including the right of reproduction in whole or in part in any form.
LITTLE SIMON is a registered trademark of Simon & Schuster, Inc., and
associated colophon is a trademark of Simon & Schuster, Inc.
For information about special discounts for bulk purchases, please contact Simon & Schuster Special Sales at
1-866-506-1949 or business@simonandschuster.com.
The Simon & Schuster Speakers Bureau can bring authors to your live event. For more information or to book an
event contact the Simon & Schuster Speakers Bureau at 1-866-248-3049 or visit our website at
www.simonspeakers.com.
Manufactured in China 0913 SCP
This Edition December 2013
2 4 6 8 10 9 7 5 3 1
Library of Congress Cataloging-in-Publication Data
Boynton, Sandra
Consider Love : its moods and many ways / written and illustrated by Sandra Boynton
p. cm.   ISBN 978-1-4422-9465-7
1. Love poetry, American. I. Title.   PS3552.O947 C6 2002   811'.54--dc21   2001034480

CONSIDER LOVE

written and illustrated by
Sandra Boynton

Little Simon

New York   London   Toronto   Sydney   New Delhi

Consider love.
Look here and there.
Consider love.
It's everywhere.
Consider love.
Observe a while.
It comes in every
shape, and style.

Szindis Zarnier
(1891-1988)
CONSIDER LOVE
oil on canvas
1937

There's simple love

and love
mysterious.

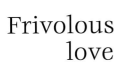

Frivolous
love

and love
too serious.

There's hopeful love

and love despairing.

Cautious love

and love that's daring.

There's
tiny love

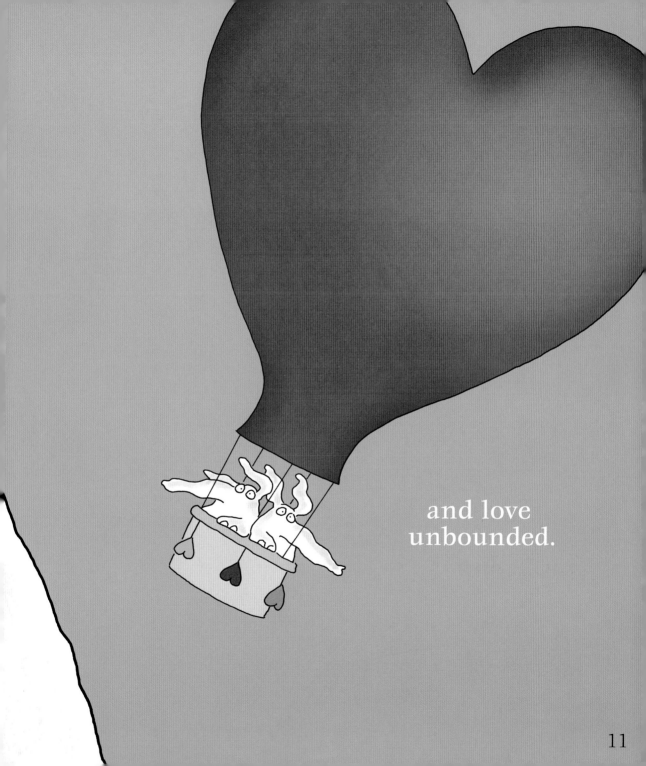

and love
unbounded.

Logical love

and love unfounded.

Love that's shallow.

Love
that's
deep.

Love  extravagant.

Love...
well, cheap.

Love that is clever.

Love
perhaps foolish.

Love oh so hot.

Love rather coolish.

Young love.

Old love.

Meek love.

Bold love.

Eloquent love

and
never-told
love.

21

Love that's inspiring.

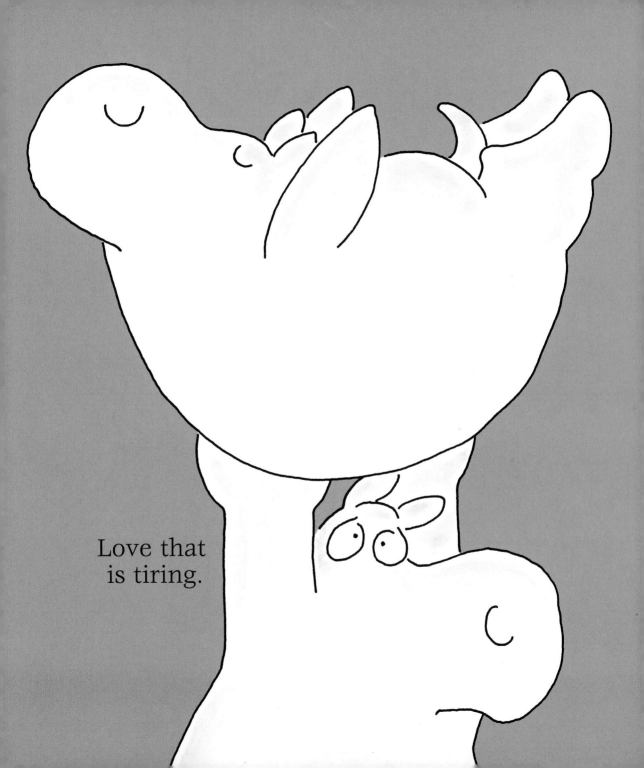

Love that
is tiring.

Love
overzealous.

Love over-jealous.

Comfortable love

and love problematic.

Love
wistful and weary.

Love gently ecstatic.

Theatrical love
that can
suffer

or smile,

make grand declarations,

and exit with style.

Now consider
one love
in the
midst of
the crowd—

an affectionate love,
neither timid nor loud.
A love that appreciates
fire, and grace.
A love that adores
one remarkable face.
A love that is
steady,
devoted,
and true—

Consider my love for incredible you.